Inside Caves

Written by Brylee Gibson

Rigby

INSIDE CAVES

All over the world there are caves.
Caves can be under the ground,
under the sea, and under the ice, too.
They can be big, or very small and narrow.

Some people like to explore caves.

under the ground

under the sea

under the ice

3

Some big underground caves have rocks that hang down, or grow up. These can take years and years to grow.

In some underground caves, there are very small animals with bright lights called glowworms. These animals use their lights to help catch their food.

stalactite

stalagmite

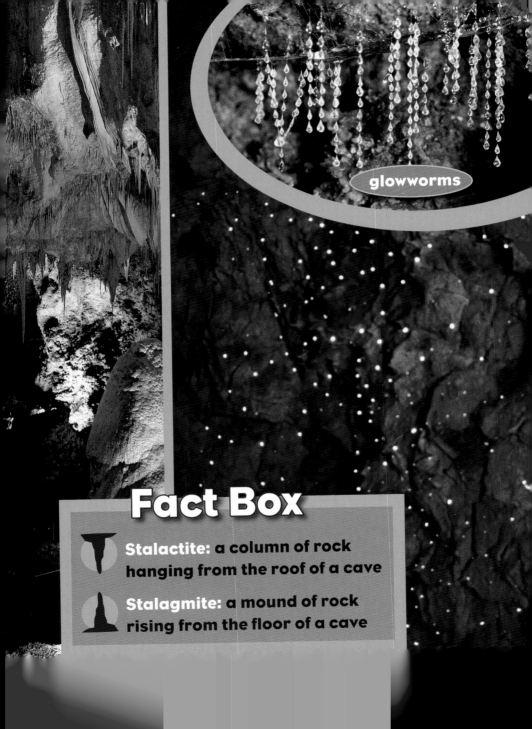

glowworms

Fact Box

Stalactite: a column of rock hanging from the roof of a cave

Stalagmite: a mound of rock rising from the floor of a cave

Some underground caves are very difficult to explore.

People must wear a helmet to protect their heads. It can be very dark in these caves, so they have a light on their helmets.

Caves in the ice are made
by water that has frozen.
In summer the caves are open, but in winter
more ice will freeze and close the caves up.
It is very, very cold inside these caves.

People who go into ice caves use
a long rope. They have to be careful
that the rope doesn't freeze.
The rope can snap if it gets too cold.
Ice could fall on their heads, so they
have to wear a helmet, too.

Caves under the water were made a long time ago. They used to be on the land, but the sea came up and filled them with water.

People who explore underwater caves
tie a rope at the start of the cave,
so they will know the way out.
They have to be careful not to kick up dirt
from the bottom of the cave.
It is hard to see where to go in dirty water.

15

People can get lost inside caves.
Cave rescuers come to rescue them
if they get lost. Cave rescuers
need to know a lot about caves.
Sometimes they have to stay in the cave
themselves for a long time.

tent

The rescuers can take snow shoes to walk on the snow and a tent in case they have to stay in the cave.

snow shoes

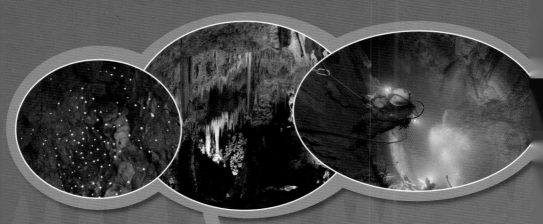

under the ground

INSIDE CAVES

under the ice

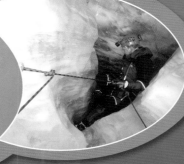

Index

under the water

Guide Notes

Title: Inside Caves
Stage: Launching Fluency – Orange

Genre: Nonfiction
Approach: Guided Reading
Processes: Thinking Critically, Exploring Language, Processing Information
Written and Visual Focus: Index, Captions, Labels, Fact Box
Word Count: 306

THINKING CRITICALLY
(sample questions)

- What do you know about caves?
- What might you expect to see in this book?
- Look at the index. Encourage the students to think about the information and make predictions about the text content.
- Look at pages 4 and 5. How do you think the glowworm's lights help it catch food?
- Look at pages 6 and 7. What do you think a helmet could protect a cave explorer's head from?
- Look at pages 8 and 9. Why do you think the caves are open in the summer?
- Look at pages 10 and 11. Why do you think the people who go into ice caves use a long rope?
- Look at pages 16 and 17. Why do you think cave rescuers sometimes stay in caves for a long time?

EXPLORING LANGUAGE

Terminology
Photograph credits, index

Vocabulary
Clarify: narrow, explore, glowworms, helmet, rescuers
Singular/Plural: cave/caves, rock/rocks, animal/animals
Homonyms: to/two/too, their/there

Phonological Patterns
Focus on short and long vowels **o** (**o**pen, gr**ow**, gl**ow**worms, r**o**pe, l**o**st, l**o**ng)
Discuss endings and root words (fill**ed**, rescu**ers**, themsel**ves**)